W9-AXF-437

ACROSS THE STREAM

BY MIRRA GINSBURG
PICTURES BY NANCY TAFURI

GREENWILLOW BOOKS · NEW YORK

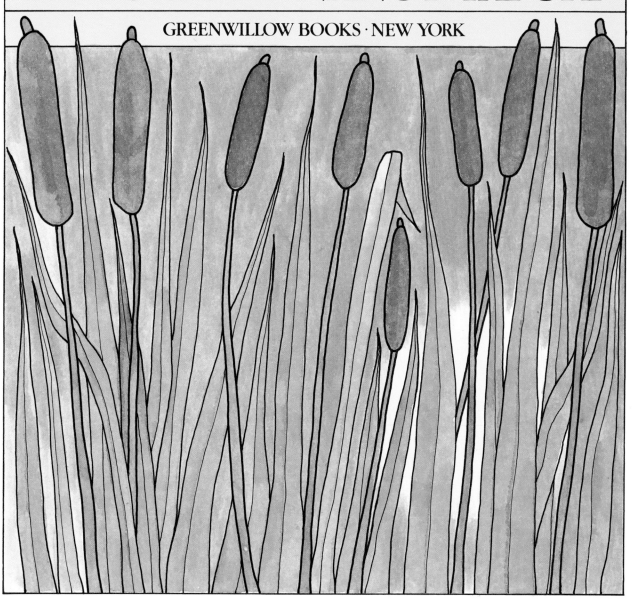

Library of Congress Cataloging in Publication Data
Ginsburg, Mirra.   Across the stream.
Summary: A hen and three chicks are saved from
a bad dream by a duck and three ducklings.
[1. Chickens–Fiction.   2. Ducks–Fiction.
3. Dreams–Fiction.   4. Stories in rhyme.]
I. Kharms, Daniil, 1905-1942.
II. Tafuri, Nancy, ill.   III. Title.
PZ8.3.G424Ac   [E]   81-20306
ISBN 0-688-01204-3   AACR2
ISBN 0-688-01206-X (lib. bdg.)

Across the Stream was inspired
by a verse of Daniil Kharms

A hen

4

and three chicks

had a
bad
dream.

8

They ran and came

to a
deep,
wide
stream.

The hen said,"Cluck, we are in luck.

I see three ducklings

and a duck."

The duck was kind,
she did not mind.

She said,"Quack,
get on my back."

They were in luck.
They crossed the stream—

a chick on a duckling,

a chick on a duckling,

a chick on a duckling,

and the hen on the duck.

And what became of

22

the bad dream?

It was left on the other side of the stream.

The End